中国诗人

女口日木
著
译

CHU

初

[汉英对照]

北方联合出版传媒（集团）股份有限公司
春风文艺出版社
·沈 阳·

## 图书在版编目（CIP）数据

初：汉英对照 / 女口日木著、译. —沈阳：春风
文艺出版社，2019.9（2021.1重印）

（中国诗人）

ISBN 978 - 7 - 5313 - 5631 - 8

Ⅰ.①初… Ⅱ.①女… Ⅲ.①诗集—中国—当代—汉
、英 Ⅳ.①I227

中国版本图书馆CIP数据核字（2019）第173044号

北方联合出版传媒（集团）股份有限公司
**春风文艺出版社**出版发行
http://www.chunfengwenyi.com
沈阳市和平区十一纬路25号 邮编：110003
永清县晔盛亚胶印有限公司印刷

| | |
|---|---|
| 责任编辑：韩　喆 | 责任校对：于文慧 |
| 装帧设计：琥珀视觉 | 幅面尺寸：125mm × 195mm |
| 印　　张：3.75 | 字　　数：82千字 |
| 版　　次：2019年9月第1版 | 印　　次：2021年1月第2次 |
| 书　　号：ISBN 978-7-5313-5631-8 | |
| 定　　价：48.00元 | |

# 自　序

　　人生没有"如果"，所以我把"如果"拆了，将"女口日木"作为自己的笔名，提醒自己：梦在前方，路在脚下。

　　《初》是我人生的首部个人中英双语诗集。诗集名取自"不忘初心，方得始终"。生活需要仪式感，三十首诗，就像三十颗珍珠，串成一册。《初》的问世，对于而立之年的我来说，绝不仅仅是个巧合，更是一种记录和激励的方式。人一生中最幸运的，莫过于做自己想要坚持做的事，爱一个恰好也爱你的人。

　　诗歌是高度凝练的文学体裁。它诞生于灵感，又离不开想象，更不能被创造，因此我一直奔走在学习的路上，乐此不疲。帘外的落花是诗、缠绵的细雨是诗、清脆的鸟啼是诗……诗歌是有生命的，那些会呼吸的文字，诱使我们张开翅膀。诗歌是有灵魂的，那些同频共振的诗行，终将引领我们诗意地生活。这是一个觉悟的过程，更是一个重生的过程。

在诗集《初》出版之际，我首先要感谢亲友和读者一直以来对我的关注与支持。感谢著名学者、诗人竺泉先生的关怀与指导。来自全国多个省市的广电主持人在第一时间受邀朗诵了我的作品，多位书画家、摄影艺术家、插画艺术家受邀创作了以本人诗歌内容为题材的艺术作品，责任编辑韩喆为诗集《初》的出版付出了大量心血，在此一并致以诚挚的谢意！

2019年1月21日

# 目　录
CONTENTS

## 不忘初心，方得始终

重回故里（组诗）        / 3

我，选择        / 6

一树花开        / 8

梅花小径        / 9

雨忆        / 10

请给我，一首歌的时间        / 12

东方水墨卷        / 13

致母亲        / 15

深与浅        / 17

筱竹听雨        / 19

旋转木马        / 20

黑土        / 22

萤火虫        / 24

# 目　录
CONTENTS

高山雪莲 / 26

景泰蓝 / 28

一个人的时光 / 29

云儿 / 30

西子之恋 / 31

问茶 / 33

你的沉默 / 34

夏日随想 / 36

拿酒来 / 37

江南小巷 / 39

一时 / 41

风月吟 / 42

风 / 43

枷锁 / 45

树的成人礼 / 47

北方·南方 / 49

# 目　录
CONTENTS

---

茶事未了　　　　　　　　　　　　　　　　/ 51

**Never forget why you started，and your mission can be accomplished**

Back to Hometown Again（a suite of poems）　/ 55

I Choose　　　　　　　　　　　　　　　/ 58

Full Tree Blossoms　　　　　　　　　　　/ 60

A Narrow Path with Plum Blossoms　　　　/ 61

The Memory about Rain　　　　　　　　　/ 62

Please Give Me a Time of Song　　　　　　/ 64

Ink Painting of Oriental Style　　　　　　　/ 66

To My Mother　　　　　　　　　　　　　/ 68

Deep and Shallow　　　　　　　　　　　/ 70

Listening to the Rain in the Bamboo Groves　/ 72

The Merry-go-round　　　　　　　　　　/ 74

The Black Earth　　　　　　　　　　　　/ 76

# 目　录
CONTENTS

| | |
|---|---|
| The Firefly | / 78 |
| Snow Lotus on the High Mountain | / 80 |
| The Cloisonne | / 82 |
| Time of Solitude | / 84 |
| A Sheet of Cloud | / 86 |
| A Love Story about the West Lake | / 88 |
| Asking Tea | / 90 |
| Your Silence | / 92 |
| Random Thoughts in Summer | / 94 |
| Bringing the Liquor | / 95 |
| Alley in the South | / 97 |
| Once in a While | / 99 |
| Romantic Chanting | / 100 |
| The Breeze | / 101 |
| The Birdcage | / 103 |
| Coming-of-age Ceremony of Tree | / 105 |

# 目 录
CONTENTS

North and South                                    / 107

An Unfinished Tea Affair                           / 109

不忘初心，方得始终

# 重回故里（组诗）

## 圆　月

月亮嫌自己胖了

便偷偷地

偷偷地

忙了一整晚

在宁静的小院儿

种下了一片雪原


## 鞋　垫　儿

你说网购方便

有人不甘

于是秉灯窗前

厚厚的茧

细细的线

绣出了一片蓝天

## 饺　子

小伙擀皮儿

姑娘和馅儿

贪玩儿的爆竹

只顾着撒欢儿

怎知那小小的湖面

扬起了叶叶白帆


## 冰糖葫芦

光阴很窄

指缝太宽

匆匆一年又溜走

雪花遮掩

细竹签

轻锁了串串珠帘

## 糖 画 儿

幸福在召唤
引众人围观
情思游走
网着半个童年
清风一飒
铸成诗一篇

## 冰 花 儿

炉火旁取暖
向南望
梅开三两点
星空无限
北风一吟
凝成画一卷

# 我，选择

假如生命是一场旅程　我
选择慢慢地度过
搭一列北上的绿皮火车
目光伸向辽阔的原野
车厢传来亲切的吆喝
过道的小推车　可还认得我？

假如生命是一条溪河　我
选择慢慢地流过
当晨曦第一缕阳光　轻吻我额头
向岸上的行人挥手
载一只舟
到汽笛声声的码头

假如生命是一季盛夏　我
选择慢慢地经过
骤雨过后
三千佳丽出水

我静静地听闻

一池荷花的开落

然而生命　远不止这些　我

选择慢慢地活

一生只专注一件事

一边行进　一边思索

在芬芳处补给

在孤独的时刻　放歌

## 一树花开

我们总是在等待

等桃花谢了又开
等燕子去了又来
等风行了十万八千里
你仍在原处徘徊

风清瘦　皱了西湖
雪痴缠　白了南山

一声鸟啼
为我带来抚慰和春的消息
等你醒来　便是一树花开

## 梅花小径

当数九的寒风
吹散了漫长的阴霾
记忆的树根　爬满青苔

是谁？是谁
在枝头，轻轻唤我？
我只身窗外
恰逢一抹幽香
在蜿蜒的小径徘徊

我驻足凝望
只见你如梦盛开
恰似一位久违的故人
踏雪而来

# 雨 忆

说实话

我并不喜欢雨

你为我撑伞

却淋湿了自己

让我在无数个飘雨的日子

想起你的呼吸

像墨西哥湾暖流

徘徊在伞的边际

让我着迷


说实话

我并不喜欢雨

没伞的时候

我们很容易成为雨的一部分

你却以伞的名义

将我揽在怀里

像平流层大气

没有雾雪云雨

给我安逸

说实话

我并不喜欢雨

雨滴敲打着玻璃

我静静地看书

你静静地看雨

我们的目光陡然相遇

像莫纳罗亚火山

喷发在沸腾的雨里

燃烧了我和你

## 请给我，一首歌的时间

漫步在微醺的海岸
你瞳孔里的浪花　在我的记忆中搁浅

我的心　是一只小小的船
一边荡漾　一边守望夜的屋檐

缱绻的流云　挣脱了时光的锁链
一会儿飞舞　一会儿遮住星星的眼

我们不念往昔　不恋风尘
只谈论海星、沙滩和诗篇

我们赤脚写字　借着昏黄的灯盏
看彼此的影子被拉成永远

清风抚弦　涌起海的呼唤
请给我　一首歌的时间

# 东方水墨卷

四月的一天
一个碧玉年华的女子
在春意绵绵的雨中
给花儿撑伞

风拂酥袖
是谁把樱花吹散
只留下绿色翅膀　迎风舒展
惹她痴心乱

雨湿羊毫
是谁在绮绘画卷
玉露中的春天　和她的素颜
或深或浅

鸟啼轻叩小伞
她优柔俯首　看了下时间
带着留恋

渐渐地走远

她的春天　她的素颜
就像她描绘的江南烟雨
一幅东方水墨卷
挂在晨暮的窗前

# 致 母 亲

你是我见过的最爱花儿的女人

当所有人都嘲笑我的梦想

只有你愿意相信

并且无条件地支持

你也有脆弱的一面

可在我面前

你永远站成一面墙


风蹉跎了你的身体

雨冲淡了你的容颜

你却用日渐弯曲的脊梁支撑着我的蜿蜒和绽放

春去秋来　花谢花开

墙越来越矮

我学会了放低姿态

在生命的最后

我借着你的温度

化作了一片芬芳的泥土

从此

每个缤纷的夏日

都绽放着似曾相识的笑脸

# 深 与 浅

幽深的森林里

小鹿乱撞

风吹过草场的感觉像浪

一排排绿色的浪

跟在浪后面的

是斑驳的阳光

不　是灯火阑珊的伪装

呼吸很绿

绿得像蓝

更像我心里流淌的旋律


你说你喜欢蓝

可你的蓝色里写着忧郁

也许只有蔚蓝的海洋

能掩藏你沉重的感伤

我挥起画笔

努力把你的蓝淡成一束光

一场心雨洒落

你的气息布满了整片森林

我小心翼翼

拾起一片被雨打湿的信笺

上面写着深深的喜欢　浅浅的悲叹

# 筱竹听雨

凭廊轻倚
看路上行人
如何撑起一首诗
穿行在雨季

风起涟漪
繁华了小溪
一只蛙　泛起荷舟
想尽情放歌　又怕你生气

筱竹轻吟
廊下的灯苗闪着
不羁的灵魂
在散落的波光里游弋

时间的旅人啊
拾起记忆里那支清瘦的笛
一曲春山夜雨
弹走了方圆三千里的孤寂

# 旋转木马

夏荷初绽　风姿优雅

在如纱的湖面上做起瑜伽

荷风轻拂　醉了繁花

朵朵笑靥摇摆着浓荫密匝


快乐园里

一只粉色木马

让我忘记了回家

我愿做你的双翼

陪你飞到天涯

也会时而把眼睛闭上

装成含羞草的模样

幻化成一枚时针

踏着时光的拍子嘀嘀嗒嗒


童声渐近

跑来两个少年

一个挎着吉他

一个抱着娃娃

一时间

我竟然分不清哪个是你

哪个是她　哪个是一朵

亭亭玉立的荷花

# 黑 土

巨大的云团在翻滚

众鸟归巢

湍急的气流在咆哮

麦浪滔滔

你矗立在风雨中

一改往日的沉默

我听见我的乳名　被你不停地叫


我抛了伞　掀了帽

冲过险滩　跨越泥淖

疯了一样朝你奔跑

我做梦也想不到

所谓的地心引力呀

竟拴不牢一颗心

所谓的千里之遥哇

竟长不过一双脚

透过熟悉的味道

我望见黑土哇——我的母亲

你焦急的目光

将我一把拽进了你的怀抱


是雨　是汗　是泪　这些都不重要

待娇红的火种点亮那云霄

我看到松花江面绽开千层笑

我听到百鸟齐鸣吹响希望的号角

# 萤 火 虫

成熟的梅子倒挂在枝头

旖旎的小山晕影在水中

是谁　如此大意

碰落了一片娇嫩的叶子

我的心　先是轻轻地痛

随后　便乘上了那只叫作叶的舟

梅子与溪流

酿成了时光的美酒

于是我醉了

我梦见一轮圆月当空

你捧着一笸相思的红豆

待我醒来

已过了半个黄昏

影子生出了叛逆

夕阳越是红啊　她就伸展得越长

炊烟学会了妩媚

风越是靠近　她就将水袖舞得越来劲

昨夜的雨声点亮了初夜之星

淡淡的　映在渐变的水中
我不由得伸出双手
捞起那久别重逢的萤火虫

# 高山雪莲

生长于高山雪线
置身云海的一朵白帆
名叫雪莲

五色的经幡　风中的祈愿
她用虔诚的目光
等待着黎明靠岸

养育了你的冰川雪水
汇成圣洁的长瀑
仿佛阿妈高高擎起的浪翠

宝石般镶嵌的海子
如此明媚
仿佛阿妹　你眼中的泉水

难怪有人转动所有的经筒
不为超度

只为触摸你的指尖

紫红色的脸
你淳朴的一笑被风舒展
仿佛一千年以前　圣山上的　那朵雪莲

# 景 泰 蓝

杏花深处　笙一曲云水蒹葭
一树芳华纷纷如雨下
却不及他纵身明朝
迷恋的盛世牡丹

庭前月下　落几笔淡墨青花
两袖月光盈盈似佳酿
却不及她梦回宫廷
斟满的绝世风雅

杨柳春风　城墙外铜胎初绽
仲夏流萤　紫铜丝以梦为马
霜叶未眠　伊人月下点红花
雪落眉间　君在瓶身烙朱砂

数流年　万般雕琢　只为它
叹韶华　半生寻觅　只为她

# 一个人的时光

一个人的时光
适合用脚步来丈量
拈指花香　小径幽长
阳光是一朵一朵的
盛开在古老的石阶上

古木幽幽　蝉声依旧
我挽着风的臂膀
却禁不住回望
那堆砌着时光的墙上
用生命写就的诗行

柔媚的小花儿
在香雾中虔诚地合掌
我徜徉在你的呼吸里
你的目光抚摸了我
往事如烟　化作袅袅梵唱
我想起经殿上
那个不慎跌倒却笑着爬起的姑娘

# 云　儿

用一朵梦的花火
燃一支哈瓦那雪茄
灵魂随烟圈儿升起
追赶一串又白又胖的鱼

她在赫本的柔情里静寂
一抹睫毛上驻泊的雪
你是白色的恋歌里
一粒粉色的心跳

你痴痴地望着云儿
一个襁褓中安睡的婴儿
风摇着她的力度刚好
我化身一只入梦的蝶

我要趁星星未醒
赴一场青屿的约
因为她在梦里说过
要将最美的嫁纱送我

## 西子之恋

桥　最懂水的柔情
你相信时光不老吗
那缠绵了千年的细吻
依然保持着最深情的姿势


鸟　最迷恋柳的娇颜
你见过倾世红妆吗
那濯发时面颊泛起的娇羞
映红了天上人间


你彷徨在水渍斑驳的石岸
感伤着墨色晕染的孤单
其实你多心了
那执着的眼和伟岸的肩
只为等候一只摇曳生姿的乌篷船


你徘徊在情丝微漾的水边
叹息着不慎滑落的美玉

却不知

那纯净的心与爱的涟漪

唤醒了一世安暖的月光


世间万物皆有灵性

哪里　有阳光、空气和水

哪里　就有不朽的爱情

# 问 茶

白鹤沐浴
常盼故人来
人间烟火散去
在沉浮之间看开

悬一壶春水高冲
潇湘妃子一笑
沉睡的玉叶
在天地之间醒来

你合上盖碗
将蝉鸣隔在窗外
出汤的玉液
在春夏之间咏怀

余香袅袅
裹挟着众生
时光哼着小调
在去留之间徘徊

## 你的沉默

慈祥的阿婆
讲述着运河开凿的动人传说
神秘的暮色
笼罩着十万人家的水岸生活
我把自己聚成一滴水的模样
静静地　听你诉说
一如你千百年来坚守的沉默
引来无数感怀的骚客

货运的船舶
在你温暖的怀里穿梭
懵懂的水鸟
从你鬓白的发际掠过
时光的电流
把你松弛的皮肤变皱
想到这里
我禁不住问你　疼吗
而你　依然选择沉默

八月的雨　来得很急

时不时在天空撕开一道道口子

所有人都匆忙躲起来了　除了你

既然这样

就让我做一只倔强的小蟹

今夜

我就是要陪你一起

在风雨中沉默地游弋

# 夏日随想

海风在树梢清唱

那些有意无意的触碰

是爱　开始的地方

于是蝴蝶展开了幻想

夏虫忘记了忧伤

一缕花香

栖落你的肩膀

踮脚仰望的时光


日落被钟声敲响

看醉梦的云霞

像少女倏然发烫的脸颊

奈何昼这么短　而夜那么长

是什么　在岁月的长河里

泛着明媚而不妖艳的光

我翻开日记

将这些细小的欢愉　收藏

# 拿 酒 来

薄暮微凉

是秋　掌起一盏小橘灯

把梦照亮


我走进一望无际的田野

看金色的麦穗上

篆刻的凝望

我舀起她目光里的湖水

饮下她的记忆

勤勤恳恳的稻草人　长大了


我来到端庄的海棠树下

看大朵的羞涩

爬满果实的脸庞

她踮起脚　靠近月亮

我听见胡琴说

默默无闻的月亮　变圆了

秋是谁　谁是秋

风月都淡了

此刻　唯一能救赎我的

怕是只有一壶老酒


拿酒来　拿最好的酒来

在落花眷恋的秋千上

永不醒来

# 江南小巷

一曲琵琶语
将小巷的温柔掬起
一柄绫罗小扇
把流云的眷恋汇聚
和风拂过思绪
我在原地转了一个圈
沐一场江南桂雨

在这样的时光里
再美的绣花鞋都是多余的
目光所及的一处风物
足以带你游走前世

在这样的巷子里
每个人都像一只归来的燕子
着一袭水墨素衣
衔一阕婉约宋词

我看见一朵落花

轻吻了另一朵落花

这是粉墙黛瓦藏不住的秘密

# 一 时

花落屋檐
一滴楚楚动人的轻叹
暗香绰影　伏案窗前
续写三生缘

琴声如诉
在精致的瓷器上回旋
夏天藏进清冽的泉眼
生出一朵莲

花向晚　琴声绵
一盏相思　两阕流年

一时
风起

风起
想你

# 风 月 吟

且问　那醉了一地的桂花
惹了谁怜
且听那斜阳箫鼓　悠扬唱段
良辰似锦声似线


且问　那言不尽的娉婷
惹了谁涟
且看她兰花云手　轻拈潋滟
亭立于隔世重逢的江南


且问　那风月花鸟一笑
惹了谁莲
且见她步若莲开　清芳初绽
折扇牡丹含羞遮面

# 风

清晨的鸟啼如洗

一盏金色的秋意

落在阳台上

盛开的书笺里

像一个暧昧的邀请

牵起我的手

穿过教堂的钟声

去收获春天里种下的爱情


我去问青鸟

可是写信的时候

他们正眉目传情

我去问白果

他们却眨着眼睛反问我

谁才是白昼里最美的星星


于是我只能在树下

默默地等你

直到我的耳际

传来阵阵纸笔相触的声音

我的裙摆洁白如云絮

你投来了又一盏秋意

我连同眼中的欣喜

从内心的麦田跃起

我要张开双翼　拥抱你

# 枷　锁

生命是何其脆弱

何其短暂

一次劫难

我便要用一生的秋天

在冰冷的枷锁中怀念

怀念蓝天　怀念山峦

怀念从你的歌声里醒来

依偎在你的身边


她赞美我的羽毛

紧接着

便撕下我身上最大的一片

只为装点她的帽檐

无数个看似平静的夜晚

却无处可逃

那只失眠的花猫

对我疯狂地纠缠

夜晚的灯光璀璨

灼痛了我的双眼

我一次次尝试

一次次盘旋

迷失在

殷红的边缘

## 树的成人礼

上一次见你

你还拼命地伸展着身体

与绮丽的云霞比高低


又一次见你

你却卸下了盛装

用金色的能量反哺大地


我原以为

只是经历了修行路上的

一场寒霜罢了

却在季风吟唱的歌剧里

被你的认真　惊异


这是你一年一度的成人礼

唯有被你深深扎根

和源源汲取的那片土地

受得起　这样的礼遇

湛蓝的天空下

我化作一只自由的海燕

贪恋着　那令我狂想的

金色的　爱的潮汐

# 北方·南方

那是广袤干燥的北方

你拉着我的手

走过春天　走过校园

走过连绵起伏的山峦

那份对待生活的热情

和对未来的憧憬

春来的山花见证了

校园的读书声见证了

漫山遍野的青松白桦也见证了

偶然看到高飞的鸿雁

你轻抚我的肩

目光宁静而深远


这是小桥流水的江南

我挽着你的手

走过秋天　走过街面

走过波光粼粼的湖畔

那份面对挫折的勇敢

和对初心的坚守

秋天的枝头见证了

街角的指示牌见证了

沿湖可见的法国梧桐也见证了

时常梦到纷飞的雪花

我便禁不住想起

你新生的白发　我北方的家

# 茶事未了

想你的时候
窗外的倦柳清瘦
风吹过来
摇曳着你的闲愁

等你的时候
桥畔的残荷白了头
雪花飘逸
像极了你的温柔

迎你的时候
我分不清大地与天空
那串长长的足印
湿润了谁的眼眸

读你的时候
袅袅茶烟氤氲了时光的音容
你我共剪一窗茶事
点缀在三月的枝头

Never forget why you started,
and your mission can be accomplished

.

# Back to Hometown Again

(a suite of poems)

## Full Moon

The moon thought she was fat

Then secretly

Secretly

She got busy the whole night

In the quiet small yard

She planted a snowfield

## Insole

You said online shopping was convenient

Someone was unreconciled

So held the lamp by the window

The thick callus

And the thin thread

Embroidered a blue sky

## Dumplings

Boys rolled the dough into wrappers
Girls mixed the fillings of dumplings
Playful firecrackers
Were enjoying themselves
How did they know on the small lake
White sails were raising

## Sugar-coated haws

Time was very narrow
The gap between fingers was too wide
A year went by quickly again
Covered by the snowflakes
The bead curtain was lightly locked
By fine bamboo sticks

## Sugar Painting

Happiness is summoning

The crowd is drawn to gather

Thoughts wander

Holding the half childhood

When a cool breeze blows

A poem is finished

## Ice Flowers

Getting warm by the fireplace

Looking to the south

Plum blossoms bloom sparsely

A star-filled sky

When the north wind songs

A painting is finished

# I Choose

If life is a journey

I choose to spend it slowly

Taking a green train to the north

The vision stretches to the vast grassland

A friendly voice comes from the carriages

The small aisle cart still recognizes me or not


If life is a river

I choose to flow slowly

When the first rays of the morning sun kisses

my forehead

I wave to pedestrians on the shore

And carry a boat

To the wharf with the sound of siren


If life is a season of summer

I choose to pass by slowly

After heavy showers

I listen quietly

A pool of lotuses blossom and fall

Just as thousands of beauties bathing


However, life is much more than that

I choose to live slowly

Concentrate on only one thing all my life

Keep thinking while moving forward

I'll promoting myself in beautiful place

And singing in loneliness

# Full Tree Blossoms

We are always waiting


Waiting for the peach blossoms to fade and blossom again

Waiting for the swallows to go and return

Waiting for the wind to cross mountains and seas

You're still prowling where you were


The thin wind creased the West Lake

The lingering snow covered the mountains


A singing of birds brings me comfort

And news of spring

When you wake up

Full tree blossoms

# A Narrow Path with Plum Blossoms

When the biting wind in winter

Blew the endless haze away

The roots of memory are overgrown with moss


Who was she

Who was calling me softly from the branches

I came outdoors

And happened to meet a fragrance

Prowling along the winding path


I stopped and stared

Just saw you blooming like a beautiful dream

Just like an old friend I haven't seen for a long

time

Arriving by snow

# The Memory about Rain

Originally

I do not like the rain

You held the umbrella for me

But got yourself soaked

It reminds me of your breath

In countless rainy days

Just like the Gulf Stream

Hovering at the edge of the umbrella

And fascinated me


Originally

I do not like the rain

When there was no umbrella

It was easy for us to be a part of the rain

You held me in your arms

In the name of the umbrella

Just like the stratosphere

Without clouds, rain, mist and snow

And gave me comfort

Originally

I do not like the rain

When the raindrops knocked on the windows

I read quietly

You watched the rain quietly

Our eyes met suddenly

Just like the Mauna Loa

Erupting in the boiling rain

And burning us

## Please Give Me a Time of Song

Walking along the slightly drunk beach

The waves in your eyes

Stay in my memory


My heart is a small boat

It keeps rippling

While looking at the edge of night


The floating cloud breaks free from the shack-
les of time

It sometimes dances

And sometimes covers the eyes of the stars


We are not addicted to the past

Nor do we fall into secularity

We just talk about starfish， beach and poetry


We write barefoot on the beach

In the dingy yellow light

Shadows of each other are stretched to infi-

nite lengths

The clear wind caresses the strings

And arouses the singing of the sea

Please give me a time of song

## Ink Painting of Oriental Style

One day in April
A girl at the age of sixteen
Held an umbrella for the flowers
In the incessant spring rain

The breeze danced her sleeves
And blew the cherry blossoms off
The tender leaves stretched like wings in the
wind
Making someone's heart ache

The rain soaked the Chinese brush
And created an ink painting
Spring in the dewdrops and her beautiful face
Or deep or shallow

The bird's singing knocked on her umbrella
She bowed her head gently

Glanced at her watch

And walked away slowly with nostalgia


Her spring and her beautiful face

Just like the misty rain in her painting

An ink painting of oriental style

Hanged to my window day and night

## To My Mother

You are the most flower-loving lady I've ever
seen
When everyone around me laughs at my dream
Only you are willing to believe it
And support me unconditionally
You are also vulnerable at times
But in front of me
You are always strong like a wall

Time made you old
Just as the wind and rain damaged the wall
But you supported my growth and blossom
With your increasingly curved spine
Seasons come and go
Flowers bloom and fade
I learned to keep a low profile
Just as the wall was getting lower and lower
At the end of life

I turned into the fragrant soil

With the influence by you


From now on

Familiar flowers bloom luxuriantly

## Deep and Shallow

Deep in the forest

When love comes

My heart races

The wind blows through the grass

Just like the waves

Rows of green waves

And following the waves

The sunshine is dappled

Just like the shining lights

The breathing is green

And the green is close to blue

Just as the melody flows in my heart


You said you liked blue

But your blue was full of melancholy

Maybe only the blue ocean could hide your

heavy sadness

I waved my painting brush

Tring to dilute your blue into a beam of light

It rained in my heart

The forest was full of your breath

With great care

I picked up a letter that was dull of wet by the
rain

Above was writing: deep love and shallow sigh

# Listening to the Rain in the Bamboo Groves

Gently leaning against the railing

Looking at the pedestrians on the path

How to walk through the rain

By holding up a poem


The water is rippled by the wind

The streamlet become passionate

A frog travels by lotus leaf in the streamlet

And wants to enjoy singing, but worries to

make you angry


The bamboo groves sing softly

The lanterns flash in the winding corridor

The free uninhibited souls

Swims in the waves of light


The time traveler

Picks up the old flute in memory

The song of night rain in spring mountain

Drives away three thousand miles of loneliness

# The Merry-go-round

Lotuses blossom for the first time

Graceful and elegant

Just like doing yoga on the gauzy lake

The breeze blows over the lotuses

The lotuses enjoy themselves

And sway their smiling faces


In the amusement park

A pink merry-go-round

Makes me forget to go home

I want to be your wings

And accompany you to the ends of the earth

Sometimes I close my eyes like mimosas

Turn myself into a clock pointer

Which ticks and ticks with the beat of time


Children's voice are approaching

Here comes two children

One carries a guitar

One holds a doll

Suddenly, I can't tell the difference

Which one is you

Which one is her

And which one is the beautiful lotus flower

## The Black Earth

The huge clouds are rolling

All birds return to their nests

The torrential air is roaring

The wheat fields roll

You stand in the storm

And change the silence of the past

I heard my infant name called by you without

interruption


I throw away the umbrella and hat

I run across the rapids and mire

Running crazily towards you

I never dream about that

The so-called gravity

Can not control a heart

The so-called mountains and seas

Are no longer than feet

Through the familiar smell

I see the black earth——my mother

Your eager eyes

Pull me into your arms


Whether it's rainwater,sweat or tears on my

face

None of these matters

After gloom comes brightness

The endless smiling faces bloom on the Song-

hua River

And the songs of countless birds brings hope

## The Firefly

Ripe waxberries covered the branches

Beautiful hills were reflected on the river

Who was so careless

Knocked off a tender leaf

My heart ached lightly at first

Then I took the boat called leaf

The waxberries and the river

Fermented into the good wine of time

I got drunk

I dreamed that a full moon hung in the sky

And you held a basket of acacia red beans

When I woke up

The sun was setting in the west

Our shadows got longer as the setting sun
got redder

The smoke danced more passionately as the
wind blew harder

The stars in the night were lit up

By the sound of rain last night

And were reflected lightly on the river

I couldn't help holding out my hands

To catch the fireflies that reunited after a long

time

# Snow Lotus on the High Mountain

Growing near the snowline of the high mountain

Just like a white sail in the sea of clouds

Her name is snow lotus


Five-colored prayer flags

Best wishes in the wind

She waits for the dawn with pious eyes


The glacier water that nurtures you

Converges into a holy waterfall

Just like the Hada held aloft by Tibetan friends


The jewel-like lake

So radiant and charming

Just like the spring water in a girl's eyes


No wonder people rotate all the prayer wheels

Not for releasing souls from purgatory

Just to touch your fingerprints


The simple smile on the purple-red face

Stretches with the wind

Just like the snow lotus on the holy mountain

a thousand years ago

# The Cloisonne

Deep in the apricot blossoms

Playing a wonderful tune with flute

Petals fall like rain by the wind

But for him

The most fascinating thing is the cloisonne of

peony in Ming Dynasty


In the moonlight garden

Drawing an aesthetic ink painting

Moonlight on the sleeves flows like good wine

But for her

The most elegant thing is the cloisonne goblet

in ancient palace


Willow twigs sway in the breeze in spring

Copper molds are being made outside the city

walls

Fireflies fly at night in summer

Copper wires are being welded with imagination

Leaves turn red after frost in autumn

She puts color on the cloisonne

Snow falls on the forehead in winter

He brands inscription under the cloisonne


Time flies

Numerous times of polishing

Just for it

Youth flies

Half a lifetime of searching

Just for her

## Time of Solitude

Time of solitude

Suitable to be measured by footsteps

The deep path is full of the fragrance of flow-

ers

The sunlight looks like flowers

Blossoming on the ancient stone steps


The dense forest is full of the chirping of cica-

das

I hold the arm of wind

But I can't help looking back all the time

On the old stone wall

The poem is written with life


The lovely flowers are devout

They fold palms together amidst the incense

in the temple

I walk in their breath

Their sight caresses me

Past events like a puff of smoke

Substituted by Buddhists' chanting

I remember the girl who fell but got up with a

smile

In the temple hall

# A Sheet of Cloud

Lighting a Havana cigar

By the kindling of dream

My soul rises with smoke

And catch up with a group of lovely fish


Immersing in Hepburn's tenderness

The snow on eyelashes

Just like a pink heartbeat

In the world of ice and snow


You look at the cloud obsessively

Just like a sleeping baby in the arms of sky

The breeze lulls her to sleep

I incarnate as a butterfly and fly in her dream


Before nightfall

Going for a romantic date

Because she told me in the dream

She would send me the most beautiful wed-

ding gauze

# A Love Story about the West Lake

Bridges understand the tenderness of water
best
Do you believe in eternal time
The kiss lingering for thousands of years
Still maintains the most affectionate posture

Birds are infatuated with willow twigs best
Have you ever seen incomparable beauty
The shyness on your cheeks in the bath
Reflects the red heaven and earth

Wandering on the wet stone shore
You feel sad for the loneliness in this ink paint-
ing
Actually, you worry too much
The persistent sight and magnanimous shoul-
ders are just waiting
For a boat with a dark awning to swing back

Lingering by the gentle waterside

You sigh at the beautiful jade that is slipped

carelessly

But you ignore

The pure heart and ripples of love

Wake up the warm moonlight of whole life


Everything has its spirituality

Where there is sunlight, air and water

There is eternal love

## Asking Tea

Cups get warm by boiling water like white
cranes bathing
I always look forward to my old friends
The earthly fireworks are dispersed
We become mature through ups and downs

Brewing tea with a pot of hot water
Just like the smiles of beauties
The sleeping tender leaves
Wake up between heaven and earth

Closing the covered bowl
Keeping the sound of cicadas outside
The tea by leaching
Sings between spring and summer

Lingering fragrance curls upwards

Encircling all sentient beings

Time sings

Hovering between going and staying

•

## Your Silence

The kind old woman

Tells a moving legend about canal digging

The mysterious twilight

Spreads across thousands of households on

both sides of the canal

I gather myself into the appearance of a drop

of water

And listen to you silently

The silence you have held for thousands of

years

Attracts a lot of sentimental poets


The freight ships

Shuttle back and forth in your warm arms

The pretty water birds

Skim over your white hair

Time goes by

And wrinkled your skin

Thought of here

I can't help asking you

Does it hurt

Yet you still choose to be silent


The rain in August arrives urgently

Every now and then lightning and thunder

Everyone takes shelter from the rain in a hur-

ry, but you

In this case

Let me be a unyielding crab

Swimming silently with you

In the storm tonight

# Random Thoughts in Summer

The sea breeze sings softly among the tree-
tops
The intentional or unintentional touch
Is the beginning of love
Butterflies begin to fantasize
Summer insects forget sorrow
A wisp of flower fragrance
Falls on your shoulders
It's the romantic time on tiptoe looking

The sunset accompanies by bells
The dreamy rosy clouds
Look like the reddish cheeks of young girls
Why the day is so short, but the night is so
long
What shines brightly and beautifully
In the long river of years
I open my diary
And collect these little pleasures

## Bringing the Liquor

It's a little cold at dusk

Autumn lights up the dream

With a small orange lamp


I walk into the endless field

So many hopeful eyes

Grow on the golden ears of wheat

I scoop up the water in their eyes

And drink their memories

The diligent scarecrow in memory is taller than

it is now


I come under the beautiful cherry-apple tree

So many faces of fruits

Are covered with shyness

They stand on tiptoe, and close to the moon

I heard huqin says

The silent moon turns round

Who is autumn? Which is autumn

Gentle breeze and bright moonlight fade away

The only thing that can save me at the mo-
ment

Is a pot of old liquor


Bring the liquor, bring the best liquor

On the swing full of falling flowers

Never wake up

# Alley in the South

A song played by lute

Holds the tenderness of alley

A small fan made of silk

Gathers the love of floating clouds

The gentle breeze kisses my mind

I turn in a circle in situ

Bathing in the rain of sweet-scented osman-

thus in the south


In such a time

No matter how beautiful the embroidered shoes

are

They are superfluous

Everything in sight

Can take you back to your previous life


In such an alley

Everyone is a returning swallow

Wearing a dress of ink

Bringing a graceful poem

A falling flower kisses another falling flower

gently

This is the secret that white walls and black

tiles can not hide

## Once in a While

A petal falls on the eaves
Just like a delicate and attractive sigh
Hidden fragrance and gentle shadow linger in
front of the window
Writing down the predestined relationship of
three lives

The sound of zither seems to be telling
Lingering on the delicate porcelain
Summer hides in a cool spring farther up
And becomes a lotus flower

The petal falls into withering gradually
The sound of zither is still going on
The same yearning between lovers
Is in different places

Once in a while, the breeze rises
The breeze rises, I miss you

## Romantic Chanting

Whose pity does the drunk sweet-scented os-
manthus cause
Just listening to the flute, the small drum and
the melodious aria
Wonderful voices are interweaved into a pic-
ture of splendid time

Whose adoration does the endless graceful
cause
Just looking at her fair orchid fingers which
bring us beautiful feelings
She seems to come from history, chanting in
the south

Which lotus blossoms caused by the agree-
able climate
Just looking at her moving in the fragrance
like a lotus in blossom
Covering her face shyly with a small peony fan

# The Breeze

Birds sing in the beautiful morning

A leaf falls in the open book on the balcony

Just like a vague invitation

It takes my hand

We go through the church bells

To reap the love planted in spring


I ask the blue birds

But they are ogling each other full of love

When the leaves fall

I ask the ginkgoes

But they ask me back with blinking

Who is the most beautiful star in the daytime


So I can only wait for you silently under the
tree

Until the rustling sound comes to my ears

My white dress raises like a sheet of cloud

Another leaf falls down

I jump from my heart field with infinite joy in
my eyes

I will open my arms to hug you

# The Birdcage

How fragile and short life is

Just one misfortune

I have to spend my whole life in the cold bird-

cage

I miss the blue sky，I miss the forest

I miss waking up from your song and snuggling

beside you


She praised my feathers

And then she tore off the biggest feather on my

body

Just to decorate her hat

In countless seemingly peaceful nights

The sleepless cat pestered me madly

But I had nowhere to run


The bright lights at night burned my eyes

I tried again and again

I circled in the birdcage again and again

But lost myself in the pool of blood

# Coming-of-age Ceremony of Tree

Once I saw you
You stretched your body as hard as you can
Comparing the height with the rosy clouds


Once again I saw you
You took off your gorgeous clothes
Feeding back the ground with golden energy


I thought it was just a frost on the way of spiri-
tual practice
However, I was shocked by your seriousness
In the opera sung by monsoon


This is your annual coming-of-age ceremony
Only the ground that you have deeply rooted
in and continuously drawn from
Can afford such a respect

Under the brilliant blue sky

I incarnate as a free petrel

And enjoy the golden waves that I yearn for

The waves are full of love

# North and South

It is the vast dry north

You hold my hand

Walking through the spring， the school yard

And the rolling hills

The passion for life and the hope for future

Are witnessed by the flowers of spring

By the sound of reading in the school yard

By pines and birches all over the mountains

and plains

Occasionally,we saw the flying birds

You caressed my shoulders gently

With serene and far-reaching sight


It is the beautiful water city in the south

I take your hand

Walking through the autumn， the street

And the sparkling lakeside

The courage to face setbacks and the adherence to original dream

Are witnesses by the fruits of autumn

By the street signs

By the French sycamores along the lakeside

Frequently,I dream of the flying snow

I can't help thinking of

Your new white hair and my northern home-

town

# An Unfinished Tea Affair

When I miss you

The willow outside the window is thin and weak

The breeze blows

Swaying your melancholy


When I wait for you

The remaining lotuses beside the bridge turn white

The snowflakes dances

Just like your tenderness


When I meet you

I can't distinguish between the sky and ground

The long string of footprints

Wet our eyes


When I read you

Time flies in the aroma of tea

We look forward to continuing the unfinished

tea affair

In March